God's
little goalkeep

Written by James Ian Campbell

Illustrated by Michael Ochelli

Editor: Alan Ferguson
Co-Editor: Patricia Campbell
Illustrator: © Michael Ochelli
Graphic Designer: Lucy Arbuthnott

With special thanks to Margaret and Pat for their helpful advise and encouragement.

Contact James Ian Campbell: jic1@btinternet.com

"I dedicate this book to my Dad, James Macleod Campbell, who sadly is no longer with us. He was a keen Hearts fan and a good player in his day, and will never be forgotten.

I also dedicate this book to my little Nephew Ben, who was born twelve weeks premature twelve years ago at the Royal Infirmary hospital in Edinburgh. Doctors didn't give him much hope of surviving, but didn't stop working to save him. It got to such a stage that a priest was called in, and was asked to baptise Ben. We prayed to God for a miracle, and mercifully, he answered our prayers.

Ben is now a big, strong boy who is a great young goalkeeper playing in the Edinburgh youth league, thanks to the miracle that was sent from Heaven twelve years ago to us: we will never forget God for sending it. God guided all the nurses and doctors through that difficult time, and they too deserve a big thank-you for not giving up on Ben.

Thank you to everyone at the Edinburgh Royal Infirmary hospital. But most of all, it's God we thank for giving life to Ben. Thank you God."

James Ian Campbell

KIDS, PLEASE SAY THE LORD'S PRAYER WITH US

The Lord's Prayer

Our Father, who lives in heaven,
Holy is your Name.
Your Kingdom come.
Your will be done on earth,
As it is in heaven.
Give us today our daily bread.
And forgive us our sins,
As we forgive those who sin against us.
And lead us not into temptation,
But deliver us from evil.
For yours is the kingdom,
The power, and the glory,
For ever and ever.
Amen.

CHAPTER ONE

Many years ago in the beautiful city of Edinburgh, Scotland, there lived a Christian boy called Joey. Joey was eleven years old and wasn't like the other boys; he was very small in size, a little bit shy, and had very few friends. All the other boys looked down on Joey when they were playing games. This upset Joey and made him sad, and often he didn't join in playing with the other boys because of this.

Now, Joey had two great loves in his life. The first one was God, and the second was football. He would pray each night to God, whom he really loved, and often talked to him late into the night. His other love was football: this love always came second to God. Joey went to a school called Leith Junior High, which was for both boys and girls aged between five and twelve years of age. It was based in the east side of Edinburgh, and was a very sporting school, with many different types of sports to choose from.

Joey liked sport: he did running, rugby, basketball, and a few others. However secretly, Joey really wanted to be the goalkeeper for his school team. Unfortunately, Joey`s size was against him because normally you had to be tall to be a goalkeeper. Sadly, to make matters worse, the school already had a very good goalkeeper called Big Eddie!

One night Joey was praying to God and asked him for something.

He said, "God, I really want to play in goals for my school team, but everyone says that I am too small to be a goalkeeper. I know that nothing is impossible for you. I know you can do all things and so I am asking you to let me be a goalkeeper for my school team. Amen."

Joey`s school had a very good football team. They had won many games during the season and managed to get to the league cup final, where they would play a school called Gorgie Junior High. This school was based across the city to the west, and always had a habit of producing great big tough teams, and this season was no different! Their team had never been beaten during the current season, which made them hot favourites to win the cup. The whole of Joey`s school were very excited about reaching the cup final, because they had never in their history got to a cup final before. Everyone at the school, including the teachers, pupils, janitor, and, of course the headmaster, were all hoping to win the cup.

Both teams were training very hard for the big match, but unknown to everyone, a disaster was about to happen for Joey`s school. Their goalkeeper big Eddie had jumped for a cross ball during a training session and fell, injuring his leg. He screamed out in great pain, then was immediately rushed to the hospital where doctors confirmed that Eddie had broken his leg. Thankfully, the doctors managed to fix him up and he was allowed to go home that night. But, sadly for him and the school, he would not play in the cup final.

Once the boys and girls at Joey`s school heard that their goalkeeper was injured and, out of the cup final they started to ask each other the question; "who`s going to go in goals now? Eddie is the best goalkeeper in the school".

During lunch time, the team got together and discussed who they could put in goals. A few names were called out, but none were suitable. Then, one boy shouted out, "What about little Joey? I know he may be small, but he is very keen, and I've seen him playing in the park. I thought he was good."

All of the other boys in the team had a long hard think about it. "Okay, let's try Joey" said one of them. Everyone nodded in agreement.

So, the next day at school, Joey was called into the headmaster's office. It was always a scary place to be. But not for Joey, because he was told he would be the goalkeeper for the school in the cup final!

"Yippee, yippee!" Shouted Joey with excitement. "I will do my best for the school and the team, I promise." Off he went, running down the corridor back to his classroom.

Joey couldn't wait for the school to finish that day, as he wanted to get home to tell his parents the good news. When he arrived home, his parents were delighted with what he had to tell them. When they heard Joey`s news, they were so proud of him that they treated him to an evening at the cinema.

In bed that night, Joey was praying to God. He said, "Thank you God, for answering my prayers and allowing me to be the goalkeeper for my school team. I knew you could make it happen for me. I love you God. Thank you again so much. Amen." He paused for a few seconds and then continued, "Oh sorry God, I forgot to say to you - would you please be with me during the cup final match? Amen."

God heard Joey`s prayer, he called two of his best angels Michael and Gabriel to his throne room. He said to them, "I want you to go down to earth and watch over little Joey during his cup final, and do not let anyone score against him."

The angels both replied, "Yes God, we will do as you have commanded."

God also said, "I will be watching his cup final, and because he loves me and prays to me everynight, I will give him a special day."

It was the day of the cup final and both teams arrived at the ground early to warm up. They checked out the pitch, and then each other. Some of the Gorgie team saw little Joey warming up and laughed at his size: they laughed even louder when they found out that Joey was the goalkeeper.

"This is going to be a easy game for us," they said. "Just look at the size of their goalkeeper, he is so small. We can't lose this final!"

Joey heard them laughing at him. He was hurt, but he ignored them and just kept on warming up. It was a nice sunny day, the pitch was in good condition, and both teams had a big support at the match. The angels that God had sent were standing behind Joey: but nobody could see them because they were invisible to the human eye. Joey didn't feel alone in his goals. He felt the presence of God was with him, and knew everything was going to be okay. It was set for a great cup final.

The Gorgie team won the toss, kicked off, and started to go forward straight away. The first low shot came towards Joey, which he saved without a problem. As the game went on, the Gorgie team were winning most of the ball. Their players were starting to build up some strong attacks but so far, after several attempts at goal, they were still unable to score. Joey was doing very well and the angels were ensuring nothing would get past him. But, after a great run down the wing from one of the Gorgie forwards, which resulted in a badly-timed tackle in the box, the referee had no option but to point to the penalty spot. Joey's defence had tried so hard to stop him but couldn't, giving away the penalty was all they could do.

"That`s the game over now. This little goalkeeper won't save this penalty," said someone in the Gorgie support.

The captain of the Gorgie team, Tricky Mickey, stepped up to take the penalty. He placed the ball on the spot, and took a long run back. He sprinted forward and hit the ball very hard. The ball was nearly in the net when the angels demonstrated their power. One of them, Michael, used his hand and lifted Joey up off the ground and directed him towards the ball. Joey caught the ball, then the angel put him safely back onto the ground. A great save from Joey!

Everyone was amazed at the save. All of Joey`s school friends were clapping and cheering and shouting his name: "Joey, Joey, Joey." Tricky Mickey was very angry with himself as it was the first penalty he had ever missed.

In the second half Joey`s team were doing really well, but struggling to score. Time and time again, both teams had good chances to win the game but no one could put the ball in the net. Each time the Gorgie players had a shot at goal; Joey was there to save it. They just couldn't score against him. People were amazed at how Joey was saving everything that came his way. The score was locked at 0-0, and extra time was looking a good possibility. Then, with only a few minutes left of the match, Joey`s team won a corner kick.

Something very strange happened at that point. Joey, who was standing in his own goal, heard a voice saying, "Joey, run up the pitch. Just start running now."

Joey knew who`s voice it was, and replied, "Yes, God", and started to run.

The angels that were with him that day gave Joey a helping hand, and gently blew him towards the opposing set of goals. It is unusual for a goalkeeper to come out of his box and run up the pitch, but it's not against the rules of the game, and had been done before.

Joey got into the opponent's box, and just as the ball

was coming over from the corner, he heard God's voice again: the words, "now jump."

He trusted in God and jumped straight into the hands of Gabriel the angel, who then lifted him higher than any of the other players could jump. With all the strength God had given him, he headed the ball powerfully into the net, and left the other goalkeeper with no chance of saving it. The crowd went wild.

"Goal, Goal, Goal! Joey`s scored!" They shouted.

The whole of Joey`s school went mad, as they clapped, cheered and danced: even big Eddie was jumping about on one leg. It was a great picture to see. Joey`s team mates picked him up off the ground and hugged him.

"Great goal. How did you manage to jump so high?" They asked.

"It was God, and I think his angels were there too. They lifted me up. It was them, I know it was them", replied Joey.

Everyone in the team was shocked at what he was saying. "Would God help us?" One boy asked.

"Oh yes, he would help any boy or girl who needed it, but you must speak to him first." Said Joey. "Sometimes your prayers may not be answered. This is when you must have faith, and never give up praying to him because he will always hear you."

There wasn't enough time for the other team to come back into the game as the whistle had gone, it was all over. Joey`s school team had won their first cup final. The crowd ran on to the pitch and lifted Joey up high

on their shoulders. He stared up at the sky and said a big thank you to God. This was a great day for him and his school. It was a final that proved that nothing was impossible for God.

After the match, as Joey`s school team were being presented with the cup, the angels Michael and Gabriel returned to heaven, where God was waiting for them in the throne room.

God said to them both, “Well done for doing as I commanded.”

The angels replied, “Yes God, we are always happy to serve you,” and went on their way to pray with Jesus.

CHAPTER TWO

Joey`s famous school cup win was seen and talked about by many football managers in the Edinburgh district. In particular there was one manager called Bob Shanks. He was a jolly kind of person, who was well known in boy's football, and considered to be one of the best managers in the city of Edinburgh. He was also the manager of the Edinburgh select school team.

Mr Shanks saw Joey play in the cup final, and was very impressed with his bravery in goals. He knew there was something different about him; something that he had never seen before, so he contacted Joey's parents and asked if Joey would come along to the trials that he was arranging. These trials were well known around the country, and had produced many famous players over the years, so it was an honour to be invited along. Joey was very happy that he was invited, but was a little bit scared as he would be up against some of Edinburgh`s best players. A total of one hundred invitations were sent out

and Joey would receive one. Only eighteen players would be picked for the squad. It was going to be tough, and Joey knew that. Nevertheless, he was looking forward to going along and playing with the other boys.

As you know, Joey`s first love was God, and Jesus too. He would talk to them every night, asking many questions. God loved to hear his questions and would listen to him all night until Joey fell asleep. One night, he said to God; "I am trying out for the Edinburgh select football team but I am so scared that I may not be good enough. What should I do?"

That night, God sent his son Jesus in a dream to Joey. In the dream, Jesus walked with him on a golden football pitch, with lines made of silver and goal posts shining brighter than diamonds. He said that he must go along to the trials, and not to be scared. Jesus then went on to say, "I will be with you on that day, I promise." The following morning, Joey woke up feeling joyful and excited. He now couldn't wait for the big day to come.

It was still a few weeks until the district trials. Joey was enjoying himself with other things. He loved going out playing with his few friends, and having long walks in the park with his dog, Bruno. One day, while out with Bruno, he was approached by some boys. One of the boys recognized Joey from the school cup final, and stopped to speak to him.

It was Tricky Mickey, the boy who missed the penalty in the final. "Are you Joey the goalkeeper?" He said.

"Yes I am", replied Joey.

"Have you been picked for the Edinburgh trials?" Asked Tricky.

"Yes, I have" replied Joey.

"So have I", said Tricky. "It will be hard to get into the team as there will be many good players there."

"I know, but I am not scared, because I've been asking God to help me, and I know he will", replied Joey.

Tricky wasn't too sure of what to say next, so he went on his way.

Joey`s parents were so proud of him and all that he had done for his school and for God, so they decided to take him on a little caravan holiday for a few days before the football trials began. Unfortunately, they had some bad news to tell him.

During the week, they had received a letter from Mr Shanks confirming that Joey was indeed invited to the district trials. But sadly, they were to be held on a Sunday. This was bad news for him because a Sunday was the day he spent with God and his family. When Joey heard the news, he started to cry. He could not believe the trials were to be held on a Sunday.

That night, Joey prayed to God and said, "Dear God, I am very sad that the football trials are to be held on a Sunday. That is our day; the day I spend with you. I will not go to these trials now, I just can't."

A little later that night, Joey cried himself to sleep, but what he didn't know was that God was only testing him. God knew how much these trials meant to Joey, and how he loved being a goalkeeper. He wanted to see if Joey loved him more than football. Secretly, God already knew the answer to that question.

The next morning, Joey said to his mum that he planned to phone Mr Shanks and tell him he couldn't make the trials as they were being held on a Sunday. So, he phoned Mr Shanks, and told him that he wouldn't be there as it was God`s day, and that he wanted to spend it with him. Mr Shanks was shocked at Joey`s decision not to come along to the trials that day but respected it nonetheless. Joey`s parents were very sad for him, but also very proud. Putting God before football was a very special thing to do for a young boy. God was watching very closely on what Joey would do, and when he saw and heard him telling Mr Shanks he wasn't going to play on a Sunday, but spend the day with God, he was so happy with him.

He said to his son Jesus, "You see that little boy down there? He has put me first before his great love of football, and passed the test I sent him. I will talk to this boy tonight."

Jesus replied, "Yes father, he has done you proud and shown great love for you. I will tell the angels to sing, celebrate, and pray for Joey".

So the angels started to sing, and bells rang out loud in heaven that night for Joey.

Later that night, Joey had a good talk with his mum and dad, then he went upstairs to his bedroom. Knowing that he was going to miss the trials was a bitter blow for him. God watched him cry that night, and so then he sent down a brilliant bright light into his bedroom.

He said, "Joey, I am so proud of you by putting me first before football. You have shown just how much you love me, and I am very happy with you. I know that you're sad missing the trials, but if you ask me, I will fix it for you: nothing is impossible for me."

Straight away, Joey asked God to fix it, and as he continued talking to him, the light slowly disappeared from the bedroom. It wasn't long after that Joey fell asleep, smiling.

The weekend had arrived and the trials were still due to be held on the Sunday. Joey was waiting for God to do something: but God doesn't rush things; his timing is always perfect. It wasn't a very nice day, so Joey decided to stay at home and invite a friend to his house to play. During the afternoon, a severe weather report came on T.V. The weatherman said that a storm was coming to the area, and that everyone should stay indoors.

Joey and his friend played most of the day, safely in his house. They didn't even notice the rain starting to fall outside: at first, it fell very lightly, then later on, very heavily. It rained all day, so much that flooding occurred in some parts of the city. Unknown to Joey, the football pitch where the trials were to be held the following day was gathering lots of water. If the rain continued, the pitches would be waterlogged and unplayable.

Well, fortunately for Joey, the rain just kept on coming down heavier and heavier; all the pitches were now covered in a foot of water. The goalposts had been blown down by the strong wind, and Mr Shanks the district manager, had no choice but to cancel the trials and re-arrange them for another day. When Joey heard that the trials had been cancelled due to the bad weather, a big smile appeared on his face, the biggest smile you have ever seen.

He knew God had fixed it for him!

"Oh thank you, God. Thank you for all the rain you have sent down today. I love you, God", said Joey.

Just then, the phone rang. It was Mr Shanks. He confirmed to Joey that the trials had been cancelled and that they were re-arranged for next Saturday.

"Will you make that day?" Asked Mr Shanks.

"Oh yes, I will be there!" Replied Joey.

After hanging up the phone, he looked up and said to God, "I will go to these trials and show them just how good a goalkeeper you have made me!"

CHAPTER THREE

The day of the district trials had arrived and Joey was there with the rest of the boys: they were all hoping to be picked for the select team. Being picked for the select team was the hardest thing Joey and the rest of the boys could do, as only the best players got to play for them. Players from all over Edinburgh were invited to show how good they really were, and Joey was one of them. Only eighteen boys would be picked for the squad, and there were at least a hundred boys who had come along so it wasn't going to be easy for him. Unknown to Joey, Jesus had kept his promise and was with him on that day. He would give Joey the strength he was going to need.

The day started well for Joey. He had been in goals and was doing very well, saving all kinds of shots and headers, and impressing the manager Mr Shanks. He felt he was becoming invincible, that nobody could score against him! Yet tiredness was creeping into Joey. He had played a lot of games during the day, but when Jesus saw this, he just blew into his face and Joey`s strength returned. Jesus

stayed with Joey during the day, watching and guiding him through every game he played.

Finally, the day came to an end. All the boys had played a lot of football, trying to impress Mr Shanks. He now had a very difficult decision to make. Just who would he pick to be his number one goalkeeper? It wasn't going to be easy as there were other good goalkeepers to choose from, and most of them were a lot taller than Joey. It was now down to Mr Shanks to call out the eighteen names who had made the squad.

Joey was very nervous. He had tried so hard to get picked, so he walked away for a few minutes to be on his own. Then he said a little prayer to God: "Thank you God for this day. Thank you God, for the way I played. It's up to you, oh God, I say; you decide, I will obey."

Mr Shanks gathered the boys around him and said, "Well done everyone. You all played your best and tried so hard, but unfortunately, I can only pick eighteen boys for the squad." He took a deep breath, and continued, "So, here are the names. I will call out your first name only, so everyone, please listen up, and no talking. Tricky, David, James, John, Daniel, Paul, Simon, Luke, Philip, Mathew, Moses, Peter, Andrew, Bartholomew, Abraham, Noah, Thomas and, for my choice in goals, Joey. I thought you were excellent in goals today, Joey, and you are now my number one goalkeeper. Well done to you all!"

When Joey got home, his Nana and Papa and all his cousins had turned up to congratulate him on making the Edinburgh select team. Joey loved having his family around. He was always happy to see them, especially his Nana and Papa who he truly loved. When visiting his Papa`s house, Joey used to watch him struggle to climb the steep stairs.

"One day Papa", said Joey, "when I make it big in football, I promise to buy you a cottage with no stairs in it."

His Papa always laughed at Joey`s words, but knew he was serious about his promise to him. He could see the kindness in Joey`s face from an early age, and knew that Joey had been blessed by God.

The first match for the Edinburgh select team was only a few weeks away, and it was against the famous Glasgow Tigers. This wasn't going to be an easy game, as the Tigers were a very strong team to play against. But, Joey wasn't bothered about their strengths because he knew no one was stronger than God – not even the Glasgow Tigers, not even a thousand Tigers!

For the next week or so, Joey put in some hard training sessions with Mr Shanks and the rest of his team mates. Mr Shanks was happy with Joey in training, and thought he would do well in the match. Then, after the final training session, the boys sat down to make arrangements to travel to Glasgow. A local bus company was booked to take the Edinburgh team through to the west. The players were to meet at the bus station at 9 a.m. on the Saturday of the match. The kick off was at 3.00pm and so they had lots of time to get through to the match.

CHAPTER FOUR

The day of the big match had arrived.

Joey was up early singing joyfully at the breakfast table, when he got a phone call from his Papa, asking if he could come over to his house for a few minutes to help him move some furniture. Joey had some time to spare so he agreed, and then went around to his Papa's house. His Papa had already started to move the furniture around when Joey arrived.

"Hello Joey, thanks for coming. Now, don't worry, I will give you a lift in my car to the bus station so you can meet up with Mr Shanks and the boys in plenty of time; if you could just help me move a few bits first", said his Papa.

"Okay", replied Joey. He helped his Papa move the furniture around the room. Joey thought he would only be there a short while, but time was soon moving on.

"Papa, look at the time. We better go now. I must be at the bus station for 9 a.m.", said Joey.

"Oh... oh, I thought you said 10 a.m.", replied Papa.

"No, 9 a.m."

"Okay then, jump into my car. It should be unlocked. I will go and get the keys. Where are my keys?" Shouted Papa.

Papa searched for the keys all over the house: upstairs, downstairs, everywhere, but he couldn't find them anywhere.

Meanwhile, Joey was getting a bit worried as he waited in the car, and time was moving on. "Hurry up Papa", he said to himself.

Then Papa remembered he had a different pair of trousers on, and his keys were in his old ones, so he searched for them everywhere.

"Where are the trousers I had on yesterday?" He asked Nana.

"I've put them in the washing machine", she replied.

"Ah, ah!" Shouted Papa, and ran to the washing machine. There, he saw his old trousers and keys going round and round in the machine.

"Oh, I must get them out! How do you stop it?" He asked Nana.

"You can't stop it until the washing has been done; it`s on a time lock", replied Nana.

"Oh no, I don't believe it", said Papa as he rushed outside to tell Joey, who was still waiting in the car.

Joey could see his Papa was upset so he didn't complain.

"Okay, I will have to run to the bus station now", he said. So off he went, running over the fields and fences to the bus station.

"Run, Joey run", shouted his old Papa.

On his way, Joey had to cross two fields; one with a big bull in it.

"Oh dear, how am I going to get across this field, with that big bull there?" Said Joey.

The bull was big and powerful, and when it saw Joey coming over the fence and into the field, it started to chase him.

"Ah! Oh! Help!" Said Joey, and ran as fast as he could over the field.

The bull was catching up with Joey, but just then, he made a very high jump over a wall and managed to get away from it.

"Wow, that was close", said Joey to himself.

Joey carried on running, and with one more field to cross, he would soon be at the station. The last field looked very easy to cross: it was flat and had long grass in it. He thought he would manage easily. But, as he started to run, he failed to notice the big hole that the farmer had dug, and he fell right in it.

"Ah! Ah! Where did that hole come from?" Shouted Joey.

He didn't see the hole as the long grass had covered it. Thankfully, he hadn't hurt himself, although he was covered in mud. Joey climbed out of the hole, and continued to run towards the station.

It was now touch and go if Joey would catch the bus, yet he still kept on running and running. God was watching down on him and admired his determination. He was tired, wet, and covered in mud. Finally, Joey got to the

bus station, but to his horror there was no bus: it had left, he had missed it. Mr Shanks and the team were unable to wait any longer and had to leave. Poor Joey just sat on the steps and cried. He couldn't believe he had missed the bus, so he started to pray to Jesus.

As he sat on the steps praying, a bus inspector saw him and wandered over.

"What`s troubling you, young man?" Said the inspector.

Joey explained to him what had happened and that he was praying to Jesus for help.

"Are you a Christian boy?" Asked the inspector.

"I am", Joey replied proudly.

"So am I", said the inspector, and he then rushed back to his office.

As Joey was just about to give up and go home, a loud voice shouted out from the depot speaker, "Bus for Joey the goalkeeper, gate number 7."

Joey heard the voice and ran to gate number 7: there waiting for him was the inspector, a driver and an empty bus.

"Is this bus for me?" Asked Joey.

"It is", replied the inspector. "You've got a football match to get to, so jump on and my driver will take you to Glasgow."

"I can't believe this, I just can't believe it", said Joey.

So he jumped on the empty bus, and started singing, dancing and cheering. It was just Joey, the driver and God that now travelled along the motorway to Glasgow. Jesus had already commanded his angels to make sure the road ahead would be clear of traffic for the bus.

Meanwhile, Mr Shanks and the team were well on their way down the motorway to Glasgow on their own bus. Everyone was disappointed that Joey wasn't with them: but just then, as Mr Shanks was looking out of the window, he saw another bus come up alongside them.

Mr Shanks glanced over to the other bus, and to his amazement, he saw Joey waving and laughing. Rubbing his eyes in disbelief, and spilling his drink down his shirt, he shouted "Eh, eh, is that Joey?"

"No, it can't be", replied Tricky.

Joey kept on waving and making funny faces at Mr Shanks and his team mates.

"Yes, it is, boys; it's Joey on that bus," said Mr Shanks.

The boys then gave the biggest cheer you've ever heard, with even Mr Shanks joining in too. Joey's bus driver peeped his horn in delight, as he caught up with Joey`s team mates. Everyone now knew that Joey was going to be in goals for the big match. Both buses arrived at the stadium at the same time, and all the boys raced up to Joey`s bus. Barely had the little goalkeeper stepped off the bus, than they were soon hugging him.

Mr Shanks looked down at Joey, smiled and said, "What a fright you gave us. But, it's nice to see you". Then he gave Joey a big football hug.

CHAPTER FIVE

It was a very hot, sunny day, and only a short time till kick off. The Edinburgh team were getting ready in the dressing room, while the Glasgow Tigers were out on the pitch, loosening up.

Mr Shanks gave the boys his final team-talk. He told them that this was going to be a hard-fought match, and that they were not to give up if they went behind in the game. When the manager finished talking, Joey said his prayer to God, and then, out they went to play the famous Glasgow Tigers.

When they got on to the park, they were booed by the majority of the crowd. Some of the Tigers' fans shouted bad words at Joey, but he didn't let it bother him. He had heard it all before. The Tigers won the toss, and picked the sun to be behind them, which meant Joey had the sun in his eyes for the first half. It was going to be difficult for him to see the ball, and everything else that was going on in the game. God was watching from above. Looking down on the match, he noticed Joey`s problem; the sun was in his eyes. So, he commanded his angels to take some clouds out of the cloud room in heaven, and cover the sun for Joey.

"Great! The clouds are covering the sun now. I can see the ball", said Joey.

Both teams were ready, and the referee blew his whistle for kick off. The match started with great pace, as some strong tackles came in from the Tigers: but the Edinburgh players weren't put off, and they soon started to pass the ball about well.

Suddenly, in the 25th minute, the Tigers' captain won the ball on the half way line. He beat two of Joey`s defenders, and shot hard at Joey`s goal. The ball was goal-bound when little Joey made a brilliant save; diving to his left, he managed to tip the ball on to the crossbar. But, unfortunately for him the ball rebounded out and fell at the feet of the Tigers' centre forward, who side footed it over the line.

"Goal, goal!" The Tigers' fans shouted.

The Tigers were now 1-0 up, and the Edinburgh defence was trying hard to hold out until half time, but were struggling to do so. Then, in the 44th minute, after another strong attack from the Tigers, they made it 2-0. Again, it was the Tigers' centre forward who did the damage, yet he looked in an off-side position. However, he was first to the loose ball, then rounded Joey and tapped the ball into the net. Joey appealed for off-side, but the linesman's flag didn't go up and so the goal stood. The Edinburgh side were now two goals down, but very glad when the referee blew his whistle for half time. Half time score: Glasgow Tigers 2- 0 Edinburgh.

In the dressing room, Mr Shanks gave his team a good talking to. He asked them not to give in and to keep trying, but he could see that their heads were down.

After he had finished talking, Joey stood up on a bench and shouted at his team mates, "Right, listen to me. Do you all believe in God?"

"Eh, yes", replied the boys.

"Okay, we need help, so let's pray to God and Jesus, and ask them both to help us in the second half."

"Okay", replied his team, and they knelt on the dressing room floor and prayed.

As they prayed, the Tigers' players made their way back to the pitch. When passing Joey's dressing room door, it was open, and the opposition players saw Joey and his mates praying. They laughed out loud.

"Ha, ha, look at those stupid fools!" Shouted one of them.

Out they came for the second half. God heard Joey and his team`s mates prayer, but was angry at what the Tigers' players had said to them as they passed Joey's dressing room door. He told his angels to gather all the clouds and bring them back into the cloud room in heaven, and because of this, it left the sun shining strongly in the eyes of the Tigers' goalkeeper. The Edinburgh team upped their game and started to win more of the ball. A brilliant one-two split the Tigers' defence wide open, allowing Edinburgh winger Tricky

Mickey to hit a powerful low shot into the Tigers' goal.

"Yes, yes! Goal! It's in!" Shouted Mr Shanks.

It was now 2-1, and Edinburgh were pressing hard for the equalizer, and it came in the 85th minute of the match. Once again, it was Tricky Mickey who produced something special. Standing on the edge of the Tigers' box, he received a long ball from his fullback. He chested the ball down, turned towards the goal in mid-air, and volleyed the ball high into the Tigers' net. The Tigers' goalkeeper was slow in seeing the ball, due to the strong sun shining in his eyes.

"Oh you beauty, what a goal!" Shouted everyone in the stadium; even the Tiger fans clapped Tricky`s goal. It was definitely the goal of the season.

Joey danced in his box, Mr Shanks fell off his chair, and the two bus drivers, who had driven Joey and his team mates through to Glasgow, tooted their horns in celebration. It was now 2-2, and only a few minutes of the match remained. The sun was still bothering the Tigers' goalkeeper, and along with a strong wind sent by God, this also made things very difficult for him.

The Tigers pushed for the winning goal and had one final shot at Joey, but he had it covered, and caught it easily in his arms. With the referee looking at his watch, Joey rushed and kicked the ball high up into the sky. The ball was carried by the wind that God had sent, and the Tigers' goalkeeper couldn't see the ball coming due to the sun in his eyes. The ball came down in his box, bounced over him and went into the net.

"Oh my", shouted Mr Shanks. "Tell me I'm not dreaming, please someone tell me! Oh Joey, I love you, my boy."

Joey had scored a miracle goal from his own box; of course, with a little bit of help from God. The referee blew his whistle, and the game was over. Edinburgh had defeated the mighty Glasgow Tigers 3-2. Both teams shook hands, and went to get showered and changed. Everyone in Joey`s dressing room was celebrating: clapping, singing and dancing. It was a great day for little Joey and his team mates. Joey hadn't forgotten about God, and sneaked away from the celebrations to be alone with him.

Joey went on to play another twelve games for the Edinburgh select, winning all of them. He was considered by many to be one of the best goalkeepers that Edinburgh had ever produced.

CHAPTER SIX

Several years had passed.

Joey was now fifteen years old and in his final few months of high school. He had only one more game to play for his school, and was told that lots of scouts from the professional clubs would be attending the match. His love for God and football was still very strong. He was now the number one goalkeeper in the city of Edinburgh, and was being watched by some of the biggest professional clubs in the country. But, there was still one small problem for Joey: his size. He was, in goalkeeper's terms, very small, and this was putting the big clubs' off making their move for him: unless Joey grew, there was little chance he would become a professional goalkeeper.

Joey had found himself a girlfriend called Mary: she was also small, but she had a big heart, and was very fond of him. Like Joey, she was a Christian girl, and would go with him to church every Sunday. Joey had also found a new friend called Robert, who had just joined Joey`s school, but he was a bit of a bad boy. He had been in lots of trouble at his last school, and had been expelled for misbehaving. He didn't believe in God and never wanted to either: he was only interested in doing wrong. No one at his school would talk to him as they were all very scared of him, but Joey always saw the best in people, and soon became close friends with Robert.

One day, on their way home from school, Robert asked Joey if he would help him steal some computer games out of a local shop.

"No way", replied Joey. "I am not doing that. Are you mad?"

Robert gave Joey an angry look and shouted, "Okay I will do it myself. You stay outside the shop."

So Joey did just that. After a few minutes, Robert came running out of the shop with some stolen games and shouted at Joey, "Run!"

Joey started to run. As they were running away from the shop, an off-duty police officer, who happened to be in the area at the time, saw both of them running and gave chase. He soon caught the boys, and then marched them to his car.

"It's down to the station for you two", he said.

"I didn't do anything. It wasn't me", pleaded Joey.

Robert just started laughing as he was dragged into the police car. When they reached the police station, Joey was very frightened and to add to his fear, he was put into a cell on his own.

He was very upset and started to cry. Praying to God, he said, "Oh God, please help me. I am in trouble. They

are saying that I stole some computer games, but you know I did not. Please help me God, as you have done in the past."

God heard Joey`s prayer and softly spoke back to him.

"Don't worry, I am with you in this cell and I will help you. I know you didn't steal the computer games. I know it was Robert."

God knew what was about to happen that day to Joey, so before the robbery, he placed an angel outside the shop disguised as a young man, who would act as a witness seeing Joey standing there. He would then go on to tell the police that Joey never went into the shop; only Robert went in and came out with the stolen games. Once the police heard what the young man (angel) had witnessed, they decided to let Joey go, but they kept Robert in jail.

The whole school had heard about what had happened to Joey. They were very angry with Robert, and decided not to talk to him or forgive him, for what he had done to Joey. Thankfully, Joey decided not to take that action as he couldn't: for he believed in God, and forgiveness is what he teaches.

Nevertheless, he was still very upset with Robert, and he needed to talk to him. So, he waited for Robert to come out of jail and return back to school. When Robert returned to school he saw Joey standing under the school shed all on his own. He went across to him and asked if they could talk.

"Yes, what is it?" Said Joey.

"I am so sorry for what I did to you. I do understand if you won't forgive me."

Joey listened carefully to what Robert had to say. Then he said, "What you did was wrong and hurtful to me, and to God. I thought you were my friend, but friends don't do that to each other. However, I do forgive you."

"You do?" Said Robert.

"Yes, I do", answered Joey.

"Are you still my friend?" Asked Robert.

"Yes, if you stop stealing from people", said Joey.

"I will", said Robert. "You are my only friend and I want to keep you as such." He couldn't believe he was forgiven, as everyone at the school hadn't forgiven him.

Robert asked Joey about God.

"Would God forgive me for all of the bad things I have done to people in the past?" He said.

"Oh yes, if you truly mean it." Replied Joey. "That is why God sent his only son, Jesus, to die on the cross for our sins. However, you must talk to him first. Why don't you come along to church with me and Mary this Sunday, and see for yourself how loving Christians are."

"Well, eh, okay; I will try it", said Robert. So, he made arrangements to meet Joey and Mary outside the church the following Sunday.

The whole school had heard that Joey had forgiven Robert, but they couldn't understand why. "How can Joey forgive Robert? It just doesn't seem right", said someone.

Joey had heard this, and spoke to them during lunch time.

"Listen, you all have brothers and sisters, don't you?" Said Joey.

"Yes," they all replied.

"And did they, at one time in your life, hurt you?" Asked Joey.

"Eh, yes", they replied.

"But, because they were your brother or sister, you forgave them, didn`t you?" Said Joey.

"Yes", they all answered again.

"Well, Robert is our brother: he did wrong, and he knows it. God says we must forgive, and that's what we must all do, forgive him", said Joey.

Everyone just looked at each other and agreed. It took a little while for Robert to be accepted by everyone at the school. But in the end, they truly did forgive him for what he done to Joey. Robert stopped stealing, and made lots of friends at school. He also kept his word to Joey, and turned up at church that Sunday.

CHAPTER SEVEN

After Joey had got over his brush with the law, he concentrated on his football.

He was now at the age where the professional clubs would be looking to sign up the best young players in the country. Joey would train nearly every night, putting most of his time into his football, and knew that a big Scottish club was watching him very closely, although he didn't know which one. He hoped, whoever they were, would make a move for him soon.

Joey's girlfriend Mary was very supportive and stood by him during the police incident that he had gone through with Robert. Mary always wanted to help people, which is why Joey liked her so much. Through the church, she and Joey would go out onto the streets to help the poor, sick, and the homeless. It was very sad seeing people living on the streets without hope, so Joey always took his bible with him; often reading parts of it to the people he met. He would also invite them along to his church, where they would receive much needed help.

One cold winter evening, Joey and Mary were out on the streets. They weren't out for long when they saw a lady, on her own; crying, and looking very confused.

"What is the matter?" Asked Joey.

"Oh, I am in a terrible mess son, but it's not your problem. Thank you for being kind and asking me anyway", said the lady.

"No, please let us help you, it's no trouble. Now, tell us what's wrong", said Joey.

The lady paused, and then explained her problem.

"Well, you see son, I was told today by my bank that I will lose my house because I can no longer afford to pay the loan. I am on my own now, and have no money to pay for it, and there`s no one to help me either", she said.

Joey and Mary were sad at hearing what she said, and decided to take her for a cup of coffee and something hot to eat. As Joey was getting the food, the lady started to talk to Mary. As she spoke, tears started to run down her face. She told Mary her name was Martha and of all her misfortunes she had gone through in her life, and how she once believed in God, but had somehow lost her way. She thought that God didn't care about her anymore.

How wrong would she be?

Joey returned with the food. He said, "Let's pray now."

Martha hesitated and said, "Okay, but I have not spoken to God for years, so he may not want to listen to me."

"Nonsense, God listens to all our prayers; at all times", said Joey.

And so, all three of them prayed to God together. They

asked him to help Martha and save her home. Martha herself cried out to God and begged him for help. High up in heaven, God listened. He remembered Martha when she was young, and how much she used to love him. He also knew that deep down in her heart, she still loved him, because he knew her very well.

After that night when Joey and Mary returned home, they started talking about Martha`s situation, and wondered if there was any way they could help her. She was over five thousand pounds in debt, which is a lot of money; but, if they could somehow find a way to raise the money, then they could help save her home.

Later that night, Joey spoke to God again. He asked God to show him the way to raise enough money to pay off Martha`s debt: God heard Joey's prayer, and was touched by his words.

That week, Joey had a tough match coming up for his high school team. It was the last match he would play for them as he was leaving soon after. He tried to focus on the match as much as possible, but he kept thinking of Martha and her problems.

Attending this match was a man called Jack Chewitt. Mr Chewitt was a tall, well built, hard-faced man from a tough part of Glasgow, and was the manager of Scottish giants, Liberty United. He had been watching Joey playing football for many years, and was aware of Joey`s height issues, but was confident that Joey would eventually grow. So, he was given the go ahead from his bosses at Liberty to sign Joey up as a professional football player that very day. Mr Chewitt wanted to watch Joey play one last time before he made his move.

The game that night proved to be a cracker. Joey had played brilliantly, making save after save. Mr Chewitt had seen enough, and that was when he made his move for Joey.

"Hello Joey", he said. "I am Mr Chewitt, manager of Liberty United. I have been watching you play football for many years now, and have been very impressed with you; so much so, that I would like to sign you up for Liberty United."

Joey went crazy with excitement!

"Yes, yes, I would like to sign for Liberty United", said Joey.

"Okay, great: but first, I need to talk to your parents; there is so much to talk about", explained Mr Chewitt.

"Okay, let's go", replied Joey.

Once they got home, Joey couldn't wait to tell his parents. He ran ahead of Mr Chewitt, and shouted to them, "I've done it, I've done it!"

"What has he done now?" Said his mother.

"I am not sure, but we`ll soon find out", replied his father.

Mr Chewitt introduced himself to Joey`s parents. They all sat down and had a long talk about Joey`s future in football. Both of Joey`s parents were very impressed with Mr Chewitt and after much discussion, they agreed to allow Joey to sign for Liberty United. Joey was soon to turn sixteen years old and on reaching that age, he would receive a big wage for playing for Liberty. When Mr

Chewitt told Joey how much money he would be getting by signing for the club, Joey nearly fell off his chair.

"Wow, that's a lot of money", said Joey.

"Yes, it is" replied Mr Chewitt.

"We will help you to look after all the money you earn until you get older", said his parents.

"Thank you, but I think I am going to need all of that money now", replied Joey.

"Why?" Asked his mother.

"Well," said Joey. "Mary and I met a lady called Martha the other night when we were out on the streets. She is ill with worry and is lost in life, and with no one to help her."

"Keep talking", said his mother.

"She stands to lose her house if she can't pay back the money to the bank, that they are demanding from her."

"How much does she owe?" Asked his father.

"Five thousand pounds", replied Joey.

"Oh dear, what a shame for her", said his mother.

Mr Chewitt was very touched by Joey`s kindness, and said to him, "What a kind boy you are. Most young boys with this sort of money would spend it on other things, like a holiday, clothes, or even a car: but you, you want to spend your first wage on saving an lady's house! I can't believe how kind you are."

"Money is not my God, and never will be. What is important to me is helping Martha to keep her house", said Joey.

"I always thought you had something different inside you Joey, and I wasn't wrong", replied Mr Chewitt.

Joey received four thousand pounds for signing a professional contract with Liberty United. That was a lot of money for Joey, but he was still one thousand pounds short of what he needed. He called up Mary and told her the good news. She was very happy that Joey had signed for Liberty United and told him not to worry, as they would find the other one thousand pounds they needed.

"We will pray to God tonight", she said.

"Yes, he will show us the way", replied Joey.

That night Joey and Mary prayed to God, saying: "God, we need your help. I have been given four thousand pounds to spend, but I want to give the money to Martha, who is in much more need of it than I am. She needs another one thousand pounds, but we don't have it. God, will you help us, so that we can help Martha? Amen."

God always liked to listen to Joey and Mary praying because they prayed from their hearts. Only time would tell if God would answer them, but I think we all know what his answer would be. God sometimes works in strange ways, and on this occasion, it was no different. He asked his son Jesus to visit Mr Chewitt in a dream. So one night, as Mr Chewitt was asleep, Jesus came to him. He told him to help Joey and Mary find the other one thousand pounds, and he placed an idea inside his head on how to do it.

Mr Chewitt woke the next morning feeling a bit strange: he remembered having a dream, but couldn't remember what it was about. Joey was on his mind all morning, and wondered if he could help him find the other one thousand pounds that the boy needed. Then, whilst having his breakfast, an idea came to him – the very idea that Jesus had placed in his head the night before.

"Oh yes, yes! Of course, why didn't I think of that before", said Mr Chewitt.

Mr Chewitt had been in the football game for many years and during that time, he had gathered some famous player's shirts. He had many of them, and these shirts were now worth a lot of money, and so Mr Chewitt decided to sell a few of the shirts on a special online collector's website. He wasn't really expecting to fetch too much for the shirts initially, but was stunned when they all sold for a very high price: the total amount was nearly two thousand pounds.

"Great. Now I can help Joey out, and give him the one thousand pounds he needs," said Mr Chewitt.

It was early in the evening when Joey received a call from Mr Chewitt.

"Hello Joey, how are you?" Said Mr Chewitt.

"Fine thanks", answered Joey.

"Guess what?" Said Mr Chewitt.

"What?" Replied Joey.

"I`ve got you that one thousand pounds that you need" said Mr Chewitt.

"What? You're kidding?" Shouted Joey with excitement.

"No, I am not kidding. I will send it over later."

"Oh… oh… thank you so much! Now I can help Martha. Mr Chewitt, I will pray for you tonight", said Joey.

"That would be nice of you, Joey, thank you. Bye for now", replied Mr Chewitt.

Joey called Mary and told her the great news that Mr Chewitt had given him.

"Oh, that's fantastic news, Joey. We can help Martha now", said Mary.

"Yes, we will try and find her tonight", replied Joey.

"Okay, see you tonight", said Mary.

That night, Joey and Mary went out onto the streets in search of Martha. They searched all the streets that they thought she may be in, but just couldn't find her.

"What will we do?" Said Mary.

"We need extra help; we need more people down here to search for her", said Joey.

So he called his friend Robert, who was at church that evening. He told Robert the situation, and explained that they needed more help in the search.

"Okay, I will bring down more people from our church, and I will call some friends from school as well", said Robert.

"Great, that's just what we need", replied Joey.

Joey had just finished talking to Robert when his mobile phone rang. It was Mr Chewitt again.

"Hello Joey", he said.

"Oh, oh, I can't talk just now as I need to find Martha before it gets dark", said Joey.

"Okay, right, I see. It looks like you need some extra help down there", replied Mr Chewitt and then hung up the phone.

Joey didn't get a chance to tell Mr Chewitt that help was on its way, so he just continued in his search for Martha.

Later in the evening, Robert turned up with lots of people to help in the search. Just as they were about to get started again, a big blue bus pulled up alongside them. The bus door sprang open. It was Mr Chewitt with a bus-load of Liberty football players.

"Okay Joey, I`ve brought some help for you", said Mr Chewitt.

Joey just laughed.

"I don't believe it, thank you", he said. "Now, let's find Martha."

Once Joey gave everyone a description of her, they split up and went different ways to find her. It was starting to get a bit dark, and Joey said a few words to Jesus.

"Jesus, please guide us to her."

They searched all over the area for her; they knew she wasn't at home, as they had knocked on her door earlier.

Mary said, "Have we tried the bowling green that closed down last year? Martha told me that is where she used to watch her husband play bowls, and how she enjoyed many happy days there."

"No, we haven't tried there yet", replied Joey.

So off they went, running to the old Bowling Green. By the time they got there, it was dark. Joey looked over the hedge, and saw a figure sitting on a bench. As he got closer, he noticed it was Martha. He found a hole in the fence and went through it; Martha sat there shivering, cold and wet.

"Hello again", said Joey.

"Oh! What a fright you gave me. What are you doing

here?" Said Martha.

"Looking for you", replied Joey.

"Me? Why, what have I done?" She asked.

"Nothing, don't worry: I have got some good news for you", said Joey.

"What is it?" Martha asked.

"We've got the five thousand pounds that you need to save your home", replied Joey.

Martha looked up at Joey in amazement and asked him, "Who sent you, young man; who really sent you?"

"Jesus. Jesus sent me", answered Joey.

Martha started to cry. She could not believe what Joey had just said to her.

"I thought Jesus had forgotten about me", she said.

"No, he has never forgotten about you: he has been with you all through your troubles, and has never left your side. Now, let's get you home", said Joey, and he took her home.

The next day, Joey accompanied Martha to the bank, where she paid the five thousand pounds into her account.

She said to the manager, "Is that all my debt paid now?"

"Yes", replied the manager.

"Great. Let's go, Joey."

Outside the bank, Joey hailed a taxi that was just passing by.

"Where to?" Said the driver.

Joey looked at Martha, and then heard her say, "To church, driver, take us to church; I've got someone to talk to."

Joey smiled and knew she meant God.

Then Martha vowed to return to God, and joined Joey`s church that very day. She would go along every Sunday, and with every Sunday that passed, she became closer to God. She was responsible for setting up a much-needed day centre for the poor and sick, and eventually became one of the leaders of the church. She never forgot how God had rescued her, nor all the help that Joey and Mary had given.

CHAPTER EIGHT

Joey was now sixteen years old and a young professional football player with a lovely girlfriend, but there was still something missing in his life. Joey couldn't understand what it was. Perhaps it was his size. He still hadn't grown much, and he did worry about it, as he didn't want to be small all his life. Yet Joey had a strong faith, and believed that, when the time was right, God would make him tall.

It was the week of Joey's debut match. He was told by Mr Chewitt that all eyes would be on him, now that he was the new number one goalkeeper. There had been a lot of talk about Joey`s size in the newspapers and on the television. Many thought he was too small: some newspapers even suggested that Mr Chewitt had made a big mistake in signing such a small goalkeeper; but Mr Chewitt never believed any of it. He always knew Joey would grow, and he was prepared to wait for that day to come. Nevertheless, all the bad press had Joey very worried.

The night before the match, he talked to Mary on the phone. She could hear in his voice he wasn't his normal self.

"What's wrong Joey?" She asked.

"Oh, I don't know. I've been thinking maybe I'm too small to be a goalkeeper. I mean, everyone is saying it; maybe they're right", replied Joey.

Mary listened. She had never heard him talk like this before, and was getting a bit worried.

"Why don't we both pray together now, over the phone?" She suggested.

"Okay" replied Joey.

They both prayed, and asked God for strength.

Mary didn't talk long on the phone to Joey that night, as she knew he had to get up early for the big match. Unfortunately, she wasn't going to be there to support him as she had some important things to do at the church. Joey was a bit sad about that, but he agreed to meet up with her later that night.

After their conversation, Joey said goodnight to his parents, and went straight upstairs to his bedroom. He jumped into his bed, and fell asleep.

During the night Joey was very restless, tossing and turning several times. His body felt unusual: he was feeling hot and sweaty all over, his legs and arms started to itch. He eventually woke up, only to find a strange white mist in his room.

"What's that?" He said to himself. "Am I dreaming?"

The mist stayed in his room for about ten minutes, and

then slowly disappeared. He tried again to get back to sleep, and finally managed to nod off.

In the morning, Joey woke up feeling great.

His mother shouted up to him, “Hurry up Joey, I’ve got your breakfast ready. It’s on the table.”

“Okay mum, be down in a minute”, he replied.

Joey went straight for his slippers, and tried to put them on his feet.

“That’s funny. I can’t get my feet into them. What’s going on?” He said.

Then, he stood up, and noticed that his pyjamas were too short for him.

“What`s happening here? First, my slippers don’t fit me, and now my pyjamas have shrunk. I don’t understand this.”

He shook his head, and reached for his dressing gown. But, as with the slippers and pyjamas, it didn’t fit. It was too small!

“Mum, Dad, come quickly”, he shouted.

Both of his parents ran upstairs to his bedroom as fast as they could.

“What is it Joey?” They asked.

“I don’t know; but all my clothes don’t fit, they are too short!” Said Joey.

“What do you mean, too short?” Said his father.

Just then, Joey stood up. His parents, now side by side with him, soon noticed that Joey stood taller than both of them. Everyone went silent. They just looked at each other in disbelief.

Looking down on them, Joey screamed, and so did his parents.

"Ah! Ah! Ah!" Everyone shouted.

"I am taller than both of you", said Joey. "How can that be? Before I went to bed last night, you two were bigger than me! What's happened?"

"You've grown Joey, you've grown my son", said both his parents, smiling with great happiness. And they all danced round the room, praising God for making him tall.

It was later in the morning, and everyone was still in shock. Joey was getting his football bag ready, when Mr Chewitt arrived. He had arranged to pick Joey up, and take him to the stadium. When he rang the door bell, Joey jokingly said to his parents, "Let me answer the door, and we'll have a laugh. I will give Mr Chewitt a fright."

"Okay, Joey", replied his mother, "This should be funny."

So Joey made his way to the door, and opened it. He looked down on Mr Chewitt, and said in a deep voice, "Hello! How are you?" (Mr Chewitt was tall himself, but Joey was now even taller).

"Eh, no, it can't be. What's happened to you, Joey?" Shouted Mr Chewitt.

"I've grown", replied Joey.

"Yes, I can see that, but how?" Said Mr Chewitt. "I saw you only yesterday, and you were small; but now you're taller than me. I don't understand it."

"Okay, I will tell you", said Joey. "You know that I am a Christian boy, and that I love God?"

"Yes, I know that", said Mr Chewitt.

"Well, in my prayers, I have always asked God to make me tall, so that I can be a goalkeeper. Last night, God must have decided that the time for me to grow had come. So, here I am", explained Joey.

"I can't believe it. It's a miracle!" Said Mr Chewitt. "You're now a perfect size to be a goalkeeper; just perfect. I am so happy for you", and he gave Joey a big football hug.

As Joey and Mr Chewitt made their way to the stadium, they both started laughing and just couldn't wait to see the look on the reporters' faces, and how they would react to Joey`s height. It was only last week that the newspapers and TV were all making fun of Joey`s size; even suggesting that Mr Chewitt had picked too small a goalkeeper for Liberty United. And so now, it would be their turn to laugh at them. But, before that, they would need to stop off at a sports shop, and buy some new boots for Joey, as his old ones were now too small for him.

Joey was now getting a little bit nervous, so he decided to give his girlfriend Mary a quick call. He had already called her earlier that morning, but couldn't get an answer. Thankfully, for Joey, she answered the phone this time.

"Hello Joey, how are you?" She asked.

"Fine. I am a little bit nervous, but otherwise, I'm okay", replied Joey. "What are you doing?"

"I am at church all day: I'm helping out, remember?" She replied.

"Oh yes, so you said. I just wanted to hear your voice before I play. I better go now, as we have just arrived at the stadium, and there are lots of reporters here. Bye for now", said Joey.

Mr Chewitt asked Joey, "Why didn't you tell her you've grown?"

"I was going to do that this morning, but now, I want to surprise her - after the match - and see the joy on her face when she sees me", answered Joey.

"Ah, okay, I understand", said Mr Chewitt.

On arriving at the stadium, their car was surrounded by waiting reporters. They all knew of Joey's small size, and were ready to give him a hard time: but, when the car doors opened, and Joey fully emerged, the reporters looked on in stunned silence.

"That can't be Joey: just look at the size of him!" Said one reporter.

"Yes. I am the new goalkeeper you've all been waiting for", replied Joey. He started to laugh at all the reporters; their faces were in shock.

Mr Chewitt couldn't stop laughing either, and fell to the ground, holding his belly.

After a few questions from the reporters, Mr Chewitt rushed Joey into the dressing room to meet up with his new team mates.

When they all saw Joey's size, they too, were stunned.

"Wow! What a height you are now; it will be great having a tall goalkeeper in goals", they said.

Joey looked down at them, and just smiled.

After getting changed and saying his prayer to God, he sprinted down the tunnel with the rest of his team. The stadium was full, and the fans were wild with excitement, as they came out of the tunnel. Joey had never heard anything like it before. There must have been at least 50,000 fans inside the stadium; the atmosphere was fantastic and Joey loved it all. Then, all of a sudden, the crowd went quiet, very quiet: so quiet, you could hear a pin drop. Everyone in the stadium was expecting to see a small goalkeeper come running out of the tunnel, but they were stunned into silence when they saw Joey.

"Is that Joey?" Said many supporters. "No, it can't be!" But, when the players' names were read out over the big speaker: "Yip, that`s Joey alright", they said, and started to sing his name.

Joey started the game well, and was forced to make some fine saves. His opponents were very strong, kicking and pushing their way through to goal, but were still unable to score against him. God hadn't sent any angels down to help Joey this time, as he wanted Joey to use the skills that he had been blessed with: however, he was watching the match from above with his son Jesus and all of the angels. Now, playing professional football is tough and, as Joey was only sixteen years old, you could expect him to make some mistakes.

And unfortunately, that's what happened to Joey: a free-kick was awarded just outside his 18-yard box. He hurriedly arranged a defensive wall, but it wasn't good enough. The shot came Joey's way with great speed, flying high into the roof of the net. Poor Joey didn't see it coming, and some of the fans shouted in anger. Joey was so sad that he hadn't saved it. Disappointed, he picked the ball out of the net, but he didn't let it bother him. For the rest of the first half, he made save after save: at half-time, Joey`s team were 1-0 behind; his fine saves had kept his team in the game.

The second half was much better for Joey and his team. They pushed hard all through that half, creating many chances, but it was only in the last ten minutes of the game that they made them count. Two late goals straight from the training ground turned the game on its head, and Joey's team were now 2-1 in front. The fans started to celebrate, but with only minutes left, they got a bit of a scare. Once again, Joey was called into action, making one last amazing save. Showing great bravery, and rushing out from his goals, he dived at the feet of his opponent, who happened to be the biggest player on the field. "What a brave save that was", shouted the crowd, and applauded Joey by clapping and cheering.

Unknown to the fans, Joey had hurt his hand. He had risked getting injured, but he had needed to make the save. Mr Chewitt made the decision to take him off a little early, and Joey made his way down the tunnel. The final whistle sounded. Joey`s team had won 2-1, and he had played a big part in the win. All his team mates were delighted; they knew he had saved them time after time during the game. The crowd went away from the stadium singing Joey's name.

He had become an instant hero to them.

CHAPTER NINE

Once Joey got into the dressing room, the club doctor checked his injured hand.

"I think you should go to hospital", he said to Joey.

"Sorry doctor, not yet; I've no time. I've got to meet my girlfriend. But, if you can strap it up for me, that would be good of you", answered Joey.

So the doctor put a bandage on Joey's hand and told him to call if it got any worse.

Joey quickly got changed and raced to meet Mary, who was still unaware that he had grown. He saw Mary sitting on a bench outside the church, and decided to tip-toe up to her.

"Hello Mary", said Joey.

Mary turned around to see Joey standing over her, tall and strong. She screamed with delight at first, then started to cry with happiness, and finally gave him the biggest hug ever.

"What's happened? What's happened? Tell me what's happened to you?" She said with great excitement.

Joey replied, "You know who has made me tall, don't you?"

"Yes, I do" she said, and continued with a prayer. "Thank you God, for making Joey tall. Thank you God, for he's not small. We love you, please hear us say, we`ll love you God, till our dying day. Amen." Then she cuddled Joey tightly.

Joey woke up the next morning with his hand still very sore, so he decided to call the club doctor, who then told him to go to hospital and get it checked out. So, off he went. On his way to hospital, his mobile phone wouldn't stop ringing. First, his old school manager Mr Shanks called, wanting to congratulate him: then it was his pal Robert, and after, many of the reporters, who all wanted to say well done to him for the way he played in his first match.

When Joey arrived at the hospital, he was met by Dr. Shake, who happened to be a fan of Liberty United. He had been at Joey`s match the day before where he had watched the young goalkeeper being taken off in pain.

Dr. Shake looked down at Joey`s hand, carefully examined it, and said, "Can I call another doctor for a second opinion?"

"Yes, no problem" said Joey.

Another doctor was called into the room.

"Hello Joey, I am Dr. Rattle", said the doctor.

"Hello", said Joey, and then had a little laugh to himself, thinking about being in a room with Dr. Shake and Dr. Rattle.

“I think we should send you to the X-ray room, Joey”, said both of them.

“Okay”, replied Joey, and off he went.

He made his way along the corridor to the X-ray room, and there waiting for him was a friendly nurse.

“Hi Joey, my name is nurse Roll”, she said.

“What? Are you kidding me?” Said Joey, and suddenly burst out laughing.

“What’s funny?” Said the nurse.

Joey explained to her.

“I was just with Dr. Shake, and Dr. Rattle. And now, you’re nurse Roll! Shake, rattle, and roll.”

He couldn’t stop laughing, as he remembered the days when his Nana sang and danced to that old song when he was a kid.

“Ha, ha! Yes, it is funny isn’t it? You’re a bit of a joker, aren’t you Joey? Now, let’s get your hand x-rayed”, said nurse Roll.

Joey waited a while in the waiting room for the doctors to come and tell him the x-ray results. Finally, they arrived, and when they did, it wasn’t good news for him. They confirmed that his hand was indeed broken.

“Oh no, not after my first game, please, no!” Said Joey.

“Sorry”, said one of the doctors. “But, it is broken, which means you won’t be able to play football for a while.”

Joey was pretty upset, he called Mary straight away. He told her the bad news. She was sad for him, and tried to cheer him up the best she could.

“Have you told Mr Chewitt yet?” She asked.

"No, not yet", he replied.

"Don't you think you should let him know?" She said.

"Yes of course; I will call him soon", replied Joey.

Mary paused for a moment, and then asked if he would come over to her house, as she had something very important to tell him. He agreed to come over later that day.

Joey`s next call was to Mr Chewitt. He told him that his hand was broken, and that he wouldn't be able to play for a while. Mr Chewitt was very disappointed for him as it was his first game.

"Of course, I could play in an outside position?" Joey joked.

"No. Just rest your hand, and I will call you later", said Mr Chewitt.

Joey returned home. He told his parents the bad news about his broken hand. They were sad for him, so his mum cheered him up by making his favourite meal of mince and tatties - a traditional Scottish meal. Despite this, he was still feeling a little bit low, and went upstairs to his bedroom to speak to God. He talked about many things that afternoon. Feeling better, he curled up and went to sleep.

Once Joey woke from his nap, and still feeling low about his broken hand, he made his way to Mary's house. On his way, he noticed a young beggar sitting in the street begging. He had holes in his shoes, no jacket, his trousers were torn, and his hair was long. He was frozen wet, and looked very sad. Everyone passed by, not wanting to stop or look at him.

But not Joey: he stopped and spoke to him.

After a quick chat, Joey said, "Right, come with me."

"Where are you taking me?" Said the beggar.

"Shopping. We're going shopping", answered Joey, and pointed to one of the largest department stores in the city.

Only the rich could afford to shop there, as it was full of the most expensive items you could ever imagine. With Joey now being a professional football player, he could easily afford to shop there. The beggar just stared at Joey and laughed out loud.

"Okay, this should be fun. When they see me and smell me, they'll run a mile!" Said the beggar.

So, in they went to the big store. As they were walking through the main door, a security man shouted out.

"Stop!"

"Who, us?" Joey asked.

"Yes, you two: stop right there."

"What is it?"

"Where do think you two are going?" Said the security man.

"Shopping", replied Joey.

"Oh no, you're not", said the security man. "This is an expensive store, and I don't think you two can afford to buy anything in here, so I think you should both leave now."

Just then, Joey reached inside his pocket, and took out a big bundle of notes, and waved them in the air.

"You see, I've got lots of money", said Joey. "And so, I can afford to shop here."

"Oh! Oh! I am sorry sir" said the security man, and he let them go on their way.

The beggar was standing there laughing. "Oh, this is great fun", he said.

All the customers in the store were looking at the beggar, shaking their heads and holding their noses.

The beggar saw them. He had a big grin on his face.

"Right," said Joey. "Let's get started. Trousers first, I think."

So, up they went to the men's department, where he bought the beggar a new pair of trousers.

"Right, now, a coat", said Joey.

He then took the beggar back down the stairs to the coat department, where he bought him a nice warm coat.

Next stop was the shoe department, where he bought the beggar a new pair of boots and a pair of thick socks.

"Have you eaten?" Asked Joey.

"No, I haven't had anything to eat for three days", answered the beggar.

"Right then, it's the restaurant for both of us!" Said Joey, where he bought the beggar the biggest meal he had ever had.

The beggar could not believe what was happening to him, and thanked Joey so much.

"May I ask you a question?" Said the beggar.

"Yes," replied Joey.

"Why have you helped me?" Asked the beggar.

"Because, you needed help. By the way, what is your name?"

"My name is Bartimaeus, Bart for short" replied the beggar.

Then Joey handed Bart some money to get a shave and haircut. He also gave him a card with his church address on it.

"I hope to see you there someday", said Joey.

"Yes, you just might", answered Bart, and gave Joey a big hug before going on his way.

God saw what Joey had done for Bart that day, and ordered celebrations in heaven.

Joey continued on his way to Mary`s house. It took a bit longer to get there, as he had spent some time helping Bart. When he arrived, Mary was already waiting at the door crying.

"What`s wrong?" Asked Joey.

"I've just been told by my father that we are moving to Africa for two years! We're going to help build a church for the local people. I don't want to leave you Joey, but I am still only fifteen years old and have no choice in the matter. I will miss you terribly", said Mary.

Joey was shocked. He couldn't take it in, and started to cry.

"No, you can't go; you can't leave me on my own. I need you here with me. Please don't go!" Cried Joey.

Mary had to do as her parents wished, and Joey knew that respecting your parent's wishes is always the right thing to do.

Eventually, Joey made his way home. Walking in the rain most of the night with his head down and crying, he tried to understand why Mary was going away. He understood there were people in some parts of Africa that needed help, and knew Mary would do well, but he still didn't want her to go.

Joey got home very late that night, and went straight upstairs to his room: he didn't even say goodnight to his parents as he was so upset. Not being his usual self, and struggling to say his prayers, Joey quickly fell asleep.

God was looking down on him, and could hear the sadness in his voice. He turned to Jesus, and said, "I must sort this out for Joey. I will fix this for him."

Joey woke the next morning, hoping that it had all been a bad dream, and that Mary wasn't going away. But, he soon realized that it was no dream, and she was leaving soon. The phone rang. He forced himself out of bed. It was Mr Chewitt.

"Hello, Joey. How's your hand?" He said.

"Still broken", answered Joey.

"Will you manage some training this week; maybe, some running?" He said.

"No. I am not going to training", replied Joey.

"Why, what's wrong?" Asked Mr Chewitt.

"Mary's leaving. She is going to spend two years in Africa with her family", explained Joey.

"Oh, that's bad news. Is there anything I can do for you?" Said Mr Chewitt.

“No, not really, but thank you for asking. I just want to be on my own for a little while”, replied Joey.

“Okay. I will call you next week. Bye for now”, said Mr Chewitt.

Joey`s parents had overheard him talking on the phone, and tried to speak to him. But, he didn’t want to talk to them, and went back into his bedroom, where he locked himself away with God for three full days. Although Joey was hurting inside, he still didn’t give up hope that Mary would stay. It was his biggest test of faith in God.

CHAPTER TEN

Joey was in such distress that he forgotten about the pain in his hand.

Unable to play football for a while, he decided to give some support to his team mates, and went along to their next match. Sitting in the stand, he looked around and listened to the fans sing, but it didn't make Joey feel any better. All he could think about was Mary. So, after the match (of which his team had lost 3-0), he met up with her.

She was still hurting, and said to him, "I wish you could come with us. My father said he would look after you, but understands you can't, due to your football career."

"Yes, I would love to go to Africa, but I've just signed a contract with Liberty, and they wouldn't be very happy if I went away", he replied.

That evening, unknown to Joey, Mary phoned Mr Chewitt.

"Hello Mr Chewitt, how are you? I was just wondering if you could spare me some of your time. I know you're a busy man, but I would like to have a talk with you", she said.

"Of course, where and when?" Answered Mr Chewitt.

"How about tomorrow at the church hall, around midday?" Replied Mary.

"Okay, see you then," said Mr Chewitt, as he wondered what Mary wanted to talk to him about.

It was the day of the meeting.

Mary had arrived early and prayed to God. She asked him for the right words to say to Mr Chewitt. She knew God would be with her.

When Mr Chewitt arrived, he looked a bit puzzled.

"Hello Mary, how are you. What`s the problem?" He asked.

Mary didn't waste any time and got straight to the point. "I want you to let Joey come to Africa with me and my family for two years. He is so unhappy at the moment. I am very worried about him", she said.

Mr Chewitt laughed out loud.

"Oh, I can't do that! Joey has a contract now: playing football is his job. It would be impossible."

"I know, but I had to ask you anyway. I am so desperate. I don't know what to do?" She said, and started to cry.

Mr Chewitt was a very tough man. He had always liked Mary, and had a soft spot for her. But sadly, this time, all he could do was watch her cry.

"I am so sorry I can't help you. I know how hard it must be for both of you, but there is nothing I can do. I better go now", said Mr Chewitt.

Before he left, God whispered in Mary`s ear: "Don't give up". So Mary decided to try one last time.

She hesitated.

"Can I ask you a couple of questions before you go?" She said.

"Yes, of course, ask away", he replied.

"Have you ever loved anyone or anything?" She asked.

"Oh yes, when I bought my little dog a few years ago. She is so beautiful."

Do you still love your dog?" Asked Mary.

"Yes, very much."

"What would you feel like, if your little dog was taken away from you, or got lost?" Asked Mary.

"I would be very sad indeed. She is all I have to keep me company at night", replied Mr Chewitt.

"Well, that`s how Joey is feeling right now, very sad", said Mary.

Mr Chewitt went silent for a few seconds. You could see him thinking.

"You are a very clever young lady, very clever indeed. I better go now, as I am running late and have a football match to watch", he said.

"Okay, thanks for coming", said Mary.

"No problem", replied Mr Chewitt, and dashed to his car.

On his way, he stopped for a moment, and thought about Mary`s words. "What a smart girl she is", he said to himself, and carried on his way.

The next day, Mr Chewitt called Joey and asked him if he would come to his office for a chat.

So Joey wasted no time, and dashed down to see Mr Chewitt. He arrived and waited outside the office, feeling a little bit nervous. After a short while, he knocked on the door.

"Come in. Hi Joey, take a seat", said Mr Chewitt.

"What is it?" Joey asked.

"How`s your hand?" Asked Mr Chewitt.

"Still broken, but on the mend. What do you want to talk to me about?"

"Well, it's like this: your girlfriend is going away to Africa and you want to go with her. Is that right?" Asked Mr Chewitt.

"Yes", said Joey.

"Okay, you can go", said Mr Chewitt.

"Eh, eh, what?" Shouted Joey.

"You can go for the two years", said Mr Chewitt.

"But what about my goalkeeping, and my contract?" Asked Joey.

"It's all sorted. You're only a young lad, and you'll have plenty of time to play football", said Mr Chewitt.

"Why are you doing this?" Asked Joey.

"Let's just say a little friend of mine convinced me yesterday that love is more important than football", he replied. "Now get out of my office before I change my mind. Your girlfriend will be waiting for you".

"Thank you so much", said Joey as he jumped over Mr Chewitt`s desk and gave him a football hug.

Joey sprinted out of the office, screaming with joy and praising God. Outside, Mary was waiting for him and saw

his smiling face. Mr Chewitt had called her earlier to tell of his decision to allow Joey to go to Africa with her. Joey couldn't believe what Mary had done for him: trying to change Mr Chewitt`s mind is an impossible task. But, she did it: she did it with the words that God had given her at that meeting.

Both of them hugged each other, looked up to God and thanked him. Then, with much happiness they shouted; "Africa, here we come YEH, YEH!!!"

THE END

JOEY TALKS ABOUT PRAYING

Hi Kids,

It is very important to pray to God. But how do you do it, I hear some of you ask. It's very simple.

If you want to pray then you can say the Lord's Prayer at the beginning of the book. This is the prayer that Jesus left for us. Or you can say your own prayer. All you have to do is talk to God in your own words .Thank him for all the things you have, like family, school, toys, games, and friends. You can talk to him at any time of the day or night because God never sleeps. When you pray to God you become close to him, which is so important, and as you pray and ask for something from God, he will decide what is best for you. God knows that some things you ask for may not be good for you, or the time isn't right. Just keep faith, and trust in him.

Myself, and Mary's prayers are not always answered, but we still talk to God every night. God loves to hear you pray to him. Prayer is very important to someone who believes in God. It's like having a direct line to your favourite footballer. Imagine if you could pick up the phone anytime of the day and talk to Messi or Ronaldo. Of course God is much, much higher than any footballer. Speaking to Messi or Ronaldo would be difficult but, speaking to God is so simple because through prayer you have a direct line to him. The one who made the world and all footballers that are in it.

You can say a prayer with your parents, brother, sister, in a group, or if you prefer, on your own. You can talk out loud, or to yourself. God doesn't mind how you talk to him. Just start by saying, Dear God.

If you have done a bad thing you can talk to God to tell him you are sorry, and ask him to forgive you. If you are really sorry then he will forgive you. God loves you, he is always there, and will always hear you, no matter what the situation is.

It took myself and Mary a few times saying the Lord's Prayer before we remembered it, but we know it well now. Why don't you go back to the beginning of the book and try it? Or say your own prayer.

See you next season, and if you're a footballer like me; play well, and practice hard.

THE JOEY INTERVIEW

"Hello, Thank you for reading the book. I hope you enjoyed it. I thought it would be good if you knew a little more about me, so I am going to answer some of your questions that you have sent me".

Q "What is your full name?"

A "Joseph James Ochelli."

Q "What is your date of birth and where were you born?"

A "I am 16 years old. I was born on 9.7.2001, in Dunfermline Fife. I moved across to Edinburgh when I was seven."

Q "Did you always want to be a goalkeeper?"

A "Yes, ever since I was born. I used to dive around my cot when I was a baby, so my dad says."

Q "Who is your favourite player, past and present?"

A "Messi, of Barcelona, for sure is the present. I would love for him to take a penalty against me. My favourite past player is former Scottish player Kenny Dalglish. I watch him all the time on You Tube. My mate Tricky Mickey, is also a favourite, he`s one to watch out for in the future."

Q “Who is your favourite manager, past and present?”

A “Mr Chewitt is my first choice. But, Sir Alex Ferguson of Manchester Utd, who is now retired, is without a doubt the greatest manager in football history. He is an ex Dunfermline Par`s player, and he is Scottish. Also Liverpool’s German manager, Jurgen Klopp is good; he has a great mind and always has good tactics.”

Q “What Scottish team do you support?”

A “That is a hard one. I support all local teams, and I think it is good for the community if a local team is doing well. But coming from Fife originally, I’d have to pick Dunfermline, and Hibs would be a close second. But, if the Hearts came in for me then, I’d be honoured to play for them”.

Q “What English team do you support?”

A “Liverpool. I hope Mr Klopp will buy me some day, I would love to play in front of the cop”.

Q “Who do your think is Liverpool`s greatest ever player?”

A “Oh that’s another tough one. There have been many great players at Liverpool over the years, but it`s Kenny Dalglish for me. My dad and papa told me all about him. (Check him out on You Tube.”)

Q "What is your favourite food and drink?"

A "I have to watch what I eat to keep fit, but my mum's mince and tatties (Scottish for Potatoes) is the best. My favourite drink is water, lots of it".

Q "Did you like school?"

A "Yes. I liked the football, but I wasn't very good at all the subjects. History and English were my best two".

Q "Do you agree it is important to listen to teachers, and do your homework?"

A "Yes and yes again. It is very important to listen to your teacher, and do as they ask. Homework is important and a big part of your education".

Q "What do you say to anyone who is being bullied?"

A "When I was at school I was bullied about my size for a while, and so I know what it is like. Tell your parents or guardian, your teacher, head teacher, club leader, big brother or sister, if you have one. Do not suffer alone; there are always people who can help you. Just talk to them. I told my teacher, and she sorted it out right away. Teachers don't stand for bullying".

Q "What is your ambition?"

A "To play for Scotland in the world cup".

Q "And finally, who is your best friend?"

A "Oh that's an easy one, JESUS is without a doubt my best friend. He has helped me so much in my young life. Without him I wouldn't be a professional footballer. If you want to know more about Jesus then just go to Google."

"I hope by answering these questions it tells you a little more about me. I will be back next year – look out for me on Amazon! Bye for now."

Joey

JESUS YOU CAUGHT MY FALL

By Joey Ochelli

Please sing with us

Verse One

Jesus Oh Jesus hear me now
Jesus Oh Jesus see me bow
Your love for me is so strong
Jesus Oh Jesus I sing this song

Chorus

Jesus Oh Jesus you caught my fall
Picked me up no matter how small
I was wrong now I know
See my face and watch it glow

Verse Two

Hope is there for all of us
Talk to him it is a must
Watch and listen to his great word
Now believe he is the Lord

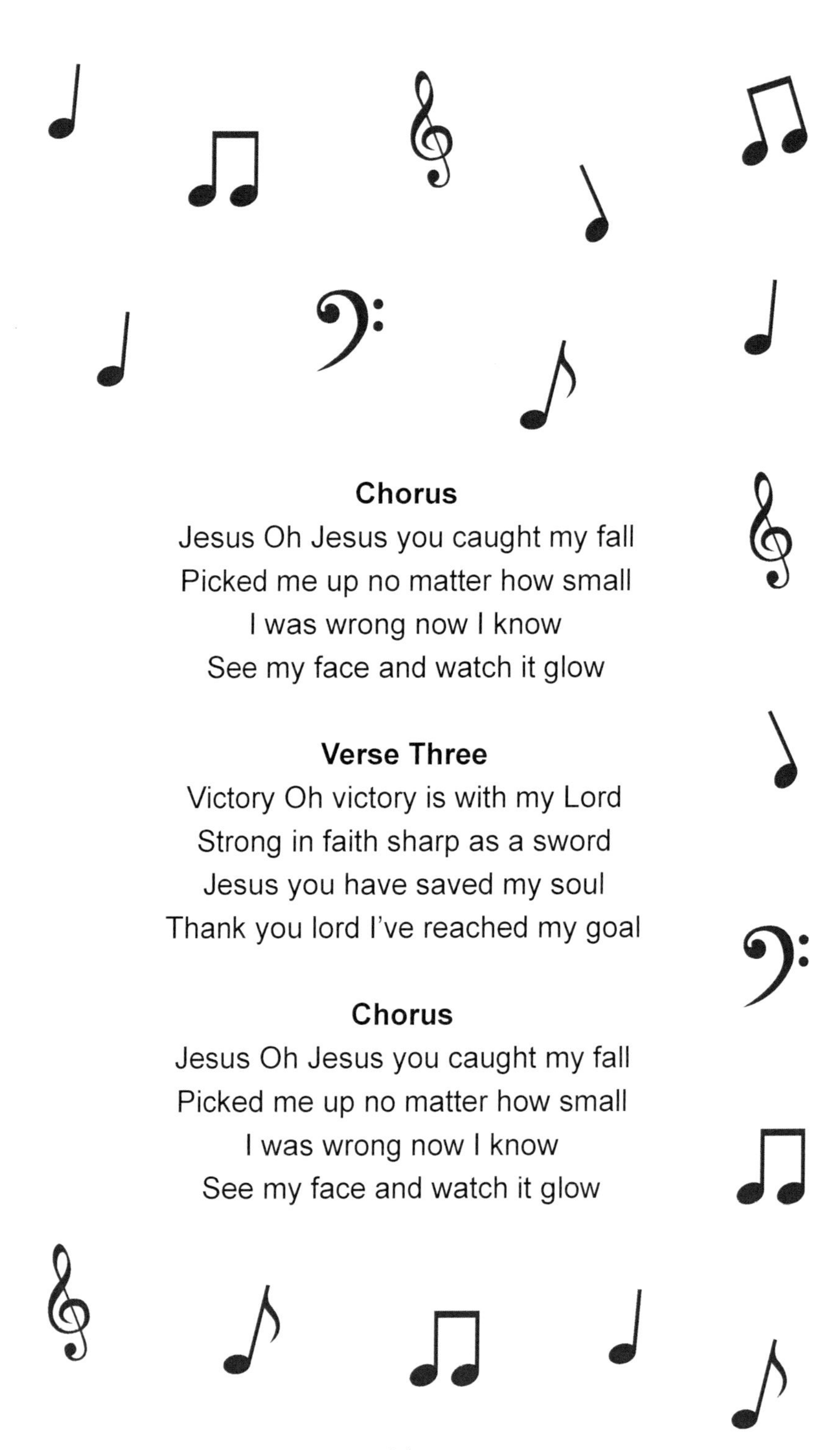

Chorus

Jesus Oh Jesus you caught my fall
Picked me up no matter how small
I was wrong now I know
See my face and watch it glow

Verse Three

Victory Oh victory is with my Lord
Strong in faith sharp as a sword
Jesus you have saved my soul
Thank you lord I've reached my goal

Chorus

Jesus Oh Jesus you caught my fall
Picked me up no matter how small
I was wrong now I know
See my face and watch it glow

Lightning Source UK Ltd.
Milton Keynes UK
UKRC02n1809310518
323546UK00019B/332